Our Big Day

Bob Johnston is the owner of The Gutter Bookshop in Dublin, Ireland. He lives in a small cottage by the sea with his husband Leon, their dog Jessie and a cat called Molly.

Originally from Boston, **Michael Emberley** has lived in Ireland for 15 years. After writing and illustrating in the US for over 40 years, this is his debut Irish children's book. Recent titles include *The Message: The Extraordinary Journey of an Ordinary Text Message*, *I Did It!* and *I Can Make a Train Noise* with Marie-Louise Fitzpatrick. He lives in an old stone horse stable in County Meath.

For Leon and Sasha

BOB JOHNSTON
ILLUSTRATED BY MICHAEL EMBERLEY

THE O'BRIEN PRESS
DUBLIN

Uncle David has lived with Simon for a very long time.
They live in a small house near the sea and they have a dog
called Bear.

When they got him as a puppy, he looked exactly like a small black bear.

But he grew up to be a very big dog.

I love going to visit Uncle David and Simon.

We take Bear for walks in the park, and sometimes to the beach to play in the sea.

Afterwards we make cakes or we do some drawing.

Bear's favourite game is 'Find it!'
I hide his ball somewhere in the garden
and then I say,
'Find it, Bear! Find it!'

Bear sniffs all around the garden until he finds the ball.

He's very good – he always manages to find it.

Uncle David and Simon are going to get married!

Everyone in the country voted to decide if two men or two women should be allowed to marry, and most of the people said 'Yes!'

So now everyone is allowed to marry the person they love the most.

Uncle David and Simon are very happy that they can finally get married.

I help Uncle David and Simon make wedding invitations.

We also make decorations to put on the wedding tables. Bear helps too, by tearing up coloured paper into small pieces to make confetti.

Uncle David and Simon ask me if I would like to be a ring-bearer with Bear at the wedding.

We will look after the wedding rings until the celebrant asks us for them.

It's a very important job.

It is the day of the wedding and all our friends and family have come to see Uncle David and Simon get married in the Grand Hotel. Everyone is dressed in their fanciest clothes.

I've got a beautiful new dress especially for the wedding. It's got a pocket to keep things in, and it will be great for twirling around in. Even Bear has a special collar, with a little bag on it to carry the ring box.

But where has the ring box gone?

It must have dropped out somewhere!

We can't have a wedding without the wedding rings.

What are we going to do?

Maybe Bear can help find the ring box, like he finds his ball in the garden?

He sniffs behind the curtains

He sniffs in Aunty Linda's handbag ...

'Find it, Bear! Find it!'

Bear sniffs under the chairs ...

... and under the tables.

He sniffs in Cousin Tom's shoes ...

but he can't find the rings anywhere!

Bear sniffs the table decorations ...

'Find it, Bear! Find it!'

He sniffs the wedding flowers ...

He sniffs in Grandad Eamonn's hat ...

He even sniffs in Granny Doreen's hair ...

but he still can't find the rings!

Bear sniffs Uncle David's trousers ...

He sniffs Simon's jacket ...

'Find it, Bear! Find it!'

He sniffs my new dress and ... he finds it!

The ring box is safe inside the little
pocket of my new dress.
It was there the whole time!

Uncle David and Simon walk down the aisle first.

Then I walk down with Bear, who carries the wedding rings on his collar.

The celebrant asks Uncle David and Simon if they will love each other and care for each other.

Uncle David says, 'Yes!'

Simon says, 'Yes!'

Then they kiss and everyone cheers. Bear is so excited that he barks too. Now they are married.

After the wedding, we have a party with lots of food and lots of dancing.

There is a big cake with a model of Uncle David and Simon and Bear on the top.

Uncle David and Simon are really happy.

Simon asks me if I would like to call him Uncle Simon now,

and I say ... 'Yes!'

First published 2022 by The O'Brien Press Ltd,
12 Terenure Road East, Rathgar, Dublin 6, D06 HD27, Ireland
Tel: +353 1 4923333; Fax: +353 1 4922777
E-mail: books@obrien.ie
Website: obrien.ie
The O'Brien Press is a member of Publishing Ireland.

Growing up with **O'BRIEN**
obrien.ie

ISBN: 978-1-78849-314-7

8 7 6 5 4 3 2 1
25 24 23 22

Printed by L&C Printing Group, Poland.
The paper in this book is produced using pulp from managed forests.

Uncle David's Wedding receives financial
assistance from the Arts Council

the arts council funding **literature**
an chomhairle ealaíon artscouncil.ie

Published in
DUBLIN
UNESCO
City of Literature